To Rebecca G and Matt M
Biggie Pals

Text and illustrations copyright © 2019 by Mo Willems.
ELEPHANT & PIGGIE is a trademark of The Mo Willems Studio, Inc.
Elephant & Piggie portrait (page 313) © 2019 by Laurie Keller.

First Edition, September 2019
10 9 8 7 6 5 4 3 2 1
FAC-029191-19172
This book is set in Century 725/Monotype; Grilled Cheese/Fontbros; Typography of Coop, Fink, Neutraface/House Industr
Printed in Malaysia
Reinforced binding

Library of Congress Cataloging-in-Publication Control Number: 2016042481
ISBN 978-1-368-04570-4

Visit www.hyperionbooksforchildren.com and www.pigeonpresents.com

An ELEPHANT & PIGGIE
BIGGIE!
Volume 2

I Am Going!
Page 3

We Are in a Book!
Page 65

I Broke My Trunk!
Page 127

Listen to My Trumpet!
Page 189

I'm a Frog!
Page 251

By Mo Willems

Hyperion Books for Children / *New York*
AN IMPRINT OF DISNEY BOOK GROUP

Originally published in January 2010.

I Am Going!

By **Mo Willems**

An **ELEPHANT & PIGGIE** Book

Hyperion Books for Children / *New York*
AN IMPRINT OF DISNEY BOOK GROUP

8

11

I am going.

PIG

20

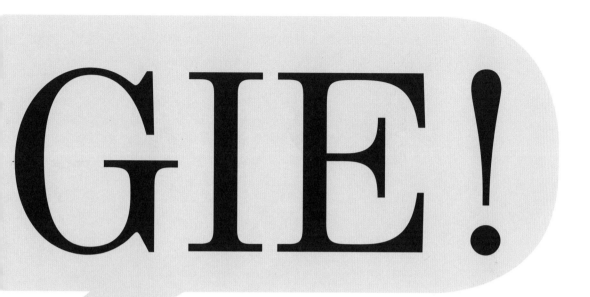

What about me?

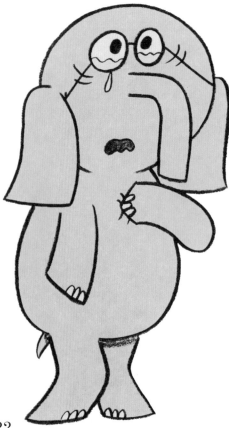

23

Who will I play
Ping-Pong with?

Who will I wear
a silly hat with?

WHO WILL I
SKIP AND
PLAY PING-PONG
IN A SILLY HAT
WITH?!?!

I am sorry,
Gerald.

Watch me go!

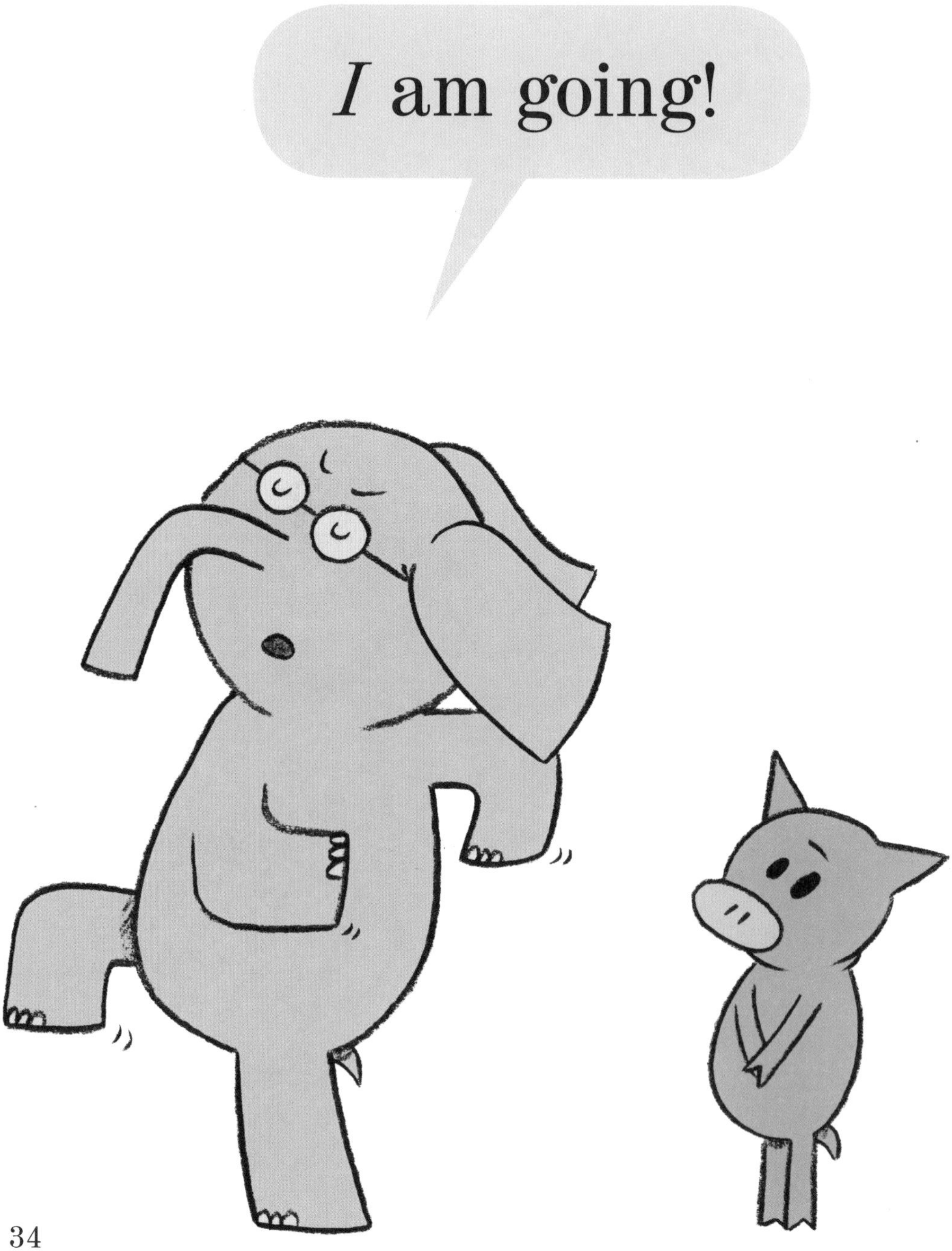
I am going!

Have fun.

41

43

Why?
Why?
Why?
Why?
Why?
Why?
Why?
Why?
Why?

Why?
Why?
Why?
Why?
Why?
Why?
Why?
Why

47

It is lunchtime,
Gerald.

Lunchtime?

I am going to
eat lunch.

54

55

Is it a *big* lunch?

59

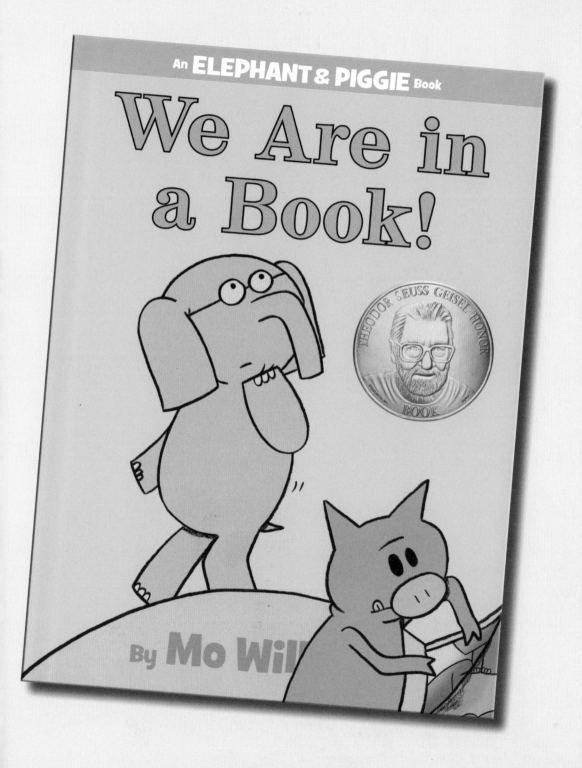

Originally published in September 2010.

An ELEPHANT & PIGGIE Book

Hyperion Books for Children / *New York*
AN IMPRINT OF DISNEY BOOK GROUP

73

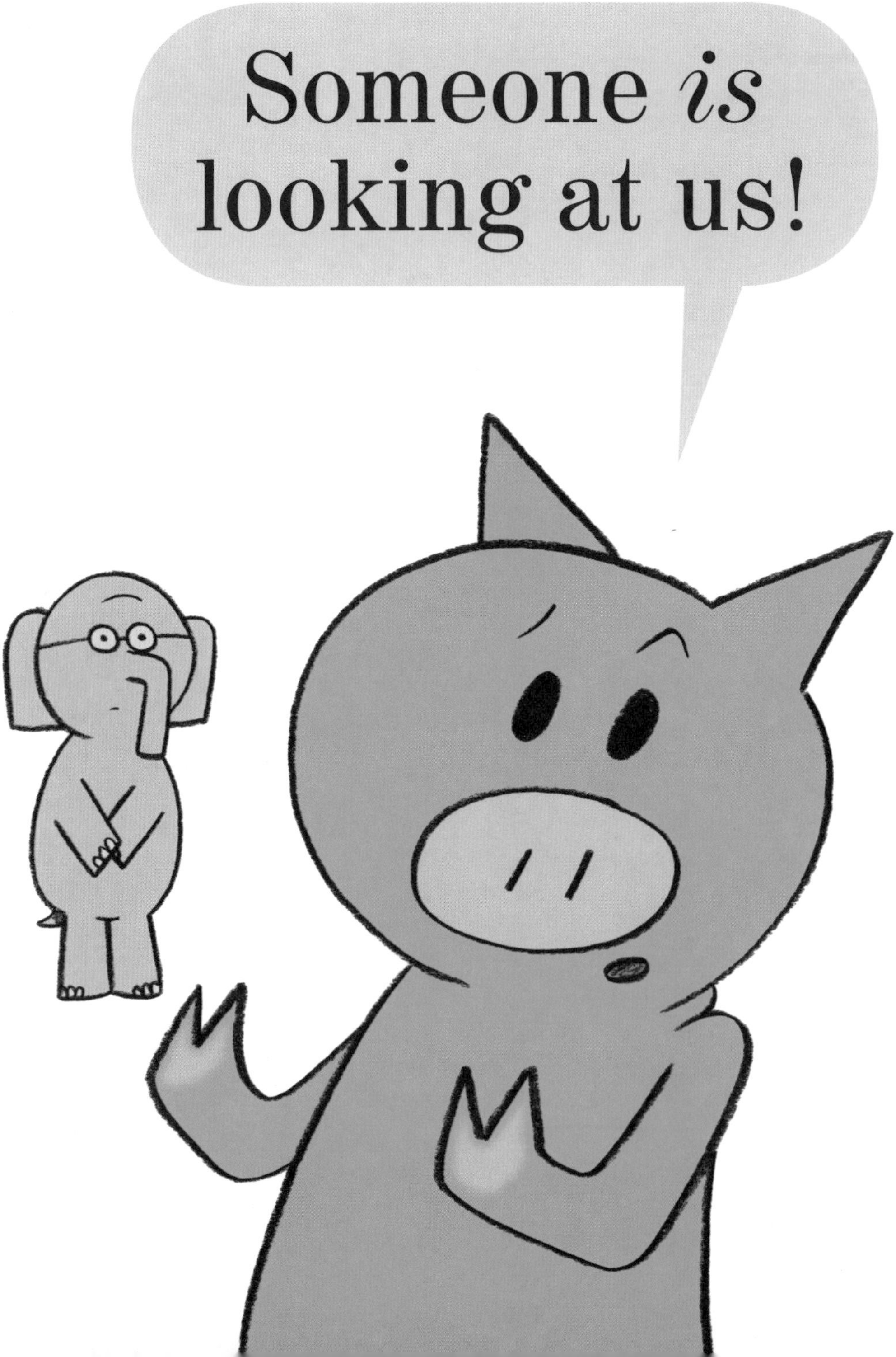
Someone *is* looking at us!

79

80

The reader is
reading these
word bubbles!

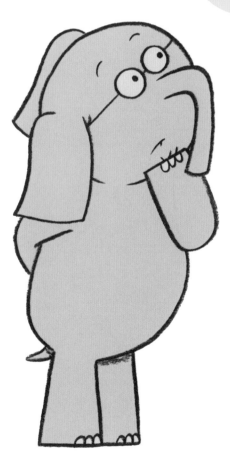

We are in
a book!

SO COOL!

If the reader
reads out loud.

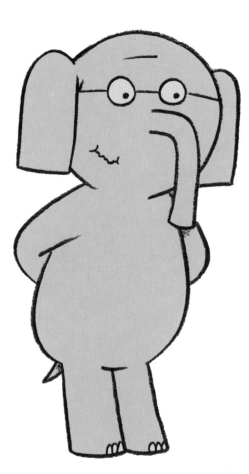

101

before the book ends?

118

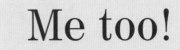

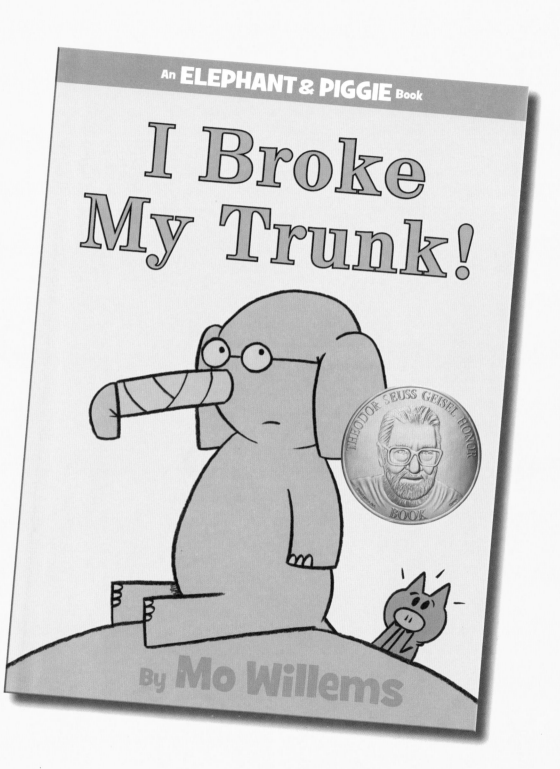

An **ELEPHANT & PIGGIE** Book

I Broke My Trunk!

THEODOR SEUSS GEISEL HONOR BOOK

By **Mo Willems**

Originally published in February 2011.

I Broke My Trunk!

By Mo Willems

An ELEPHANT & PIGGIE Book

Hyperion Books for Children / *New York*
AN IMPRINT OF DISNEY BOOK GROUP

I have not seen
Gerald today.

Why?

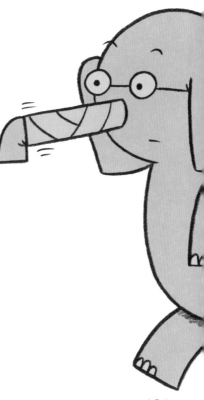

137

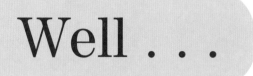
Well . . .

I was playing
with Hippo.

138

Then, I had an idea!
I wanted to lift Hippo
onto my trunk!

So, I lifted Hippo onto my trunk.

144

There is more
to my story.

149

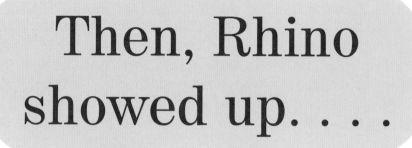

Rhino wanted a turn.

What did
you do?

155

But, a hippo *and* a rhino on your trunk are very heavy.

172

173

Well, I was so proud of
what I had done . . .

that I ran to tell my very best friend about it!

177

179

180

WHOOP!

183

It is a long,
crazy story. . . .

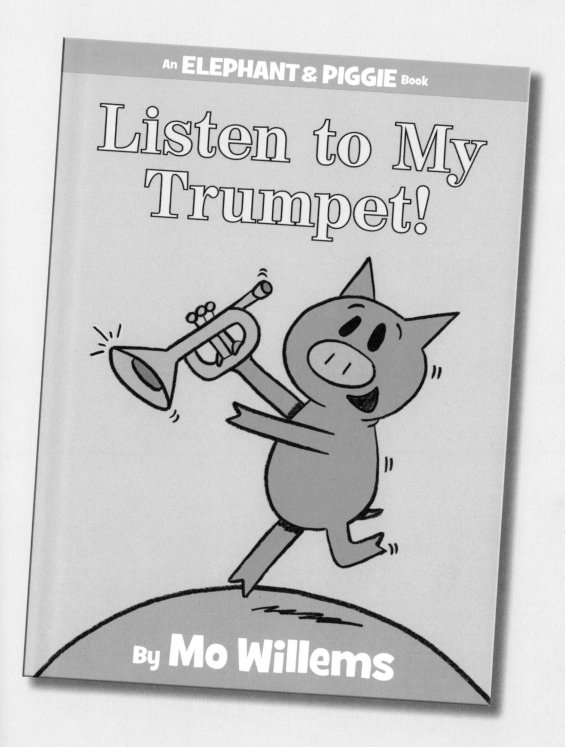

Originally published in February 2012

By

Mo Willems

Listen to My Trumpet!

An ELEPHANT & PIGGIE Book

Hyperion Books for Children / *New York*

AN IMPRINT OF DISNEY BOOK GROUP

Do not move!

195

MMMM! MMMM! MMMM!

MMMM!

202

209

211

And now the
BIG FINISH!

Finished!

225

You, uh, hold your trumpet very well.

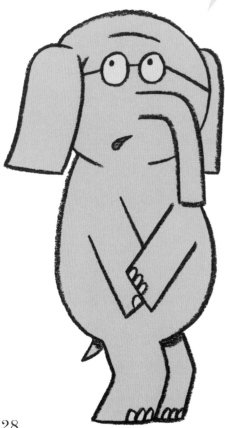

I'm waiting. . . .

Piggie. You are my friend.

And I am
your friend.

So, I will tell
you the truth.

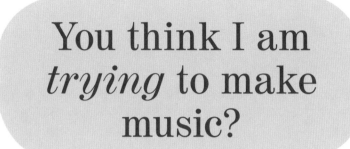

240

241

245

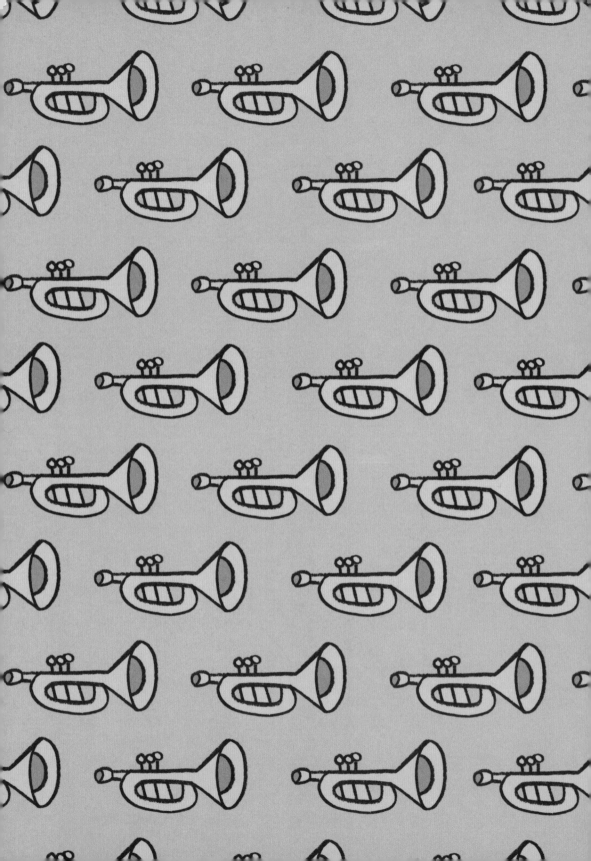

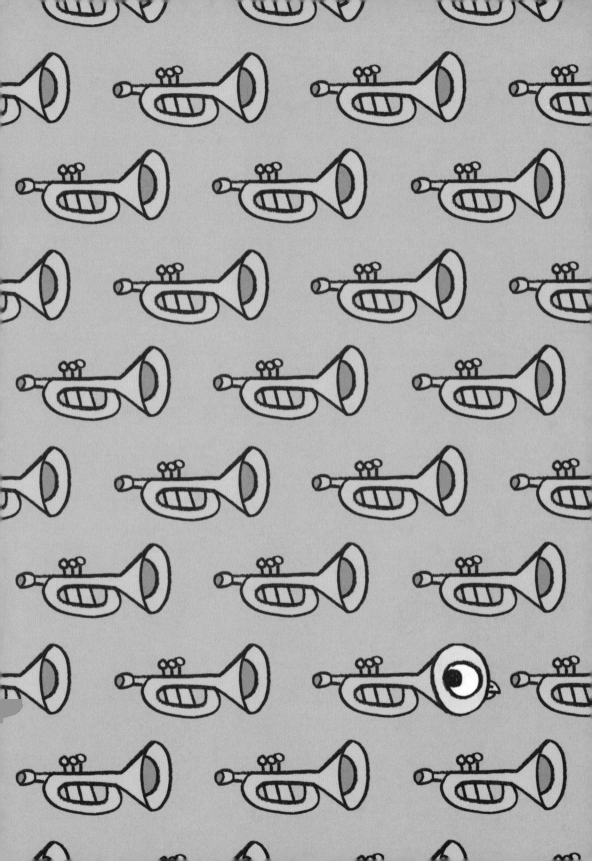

Originally published in October 2013.

An ELEPHANT & PIGGIE Book

Hyperion Books for Children
New York
AN IMPRINT OF DISNEY BOOK GROUP

Ribbit!

259

261

I was sure
you were a pig.

267

269

271

Ribbit!

I DO NOT
TO BE A

281

282

284

287

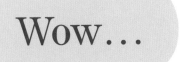

All the time.

295

297

298

No, I
can't!

Yes,
you can!

No, I
can't!

No, I
can't!

Yes,
you can!

No, I
can't!

No, I
can't!

Yes,
you can!

303

Why can't you
pretend to be
a frog!?

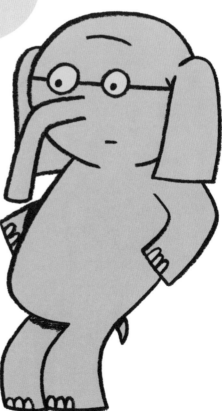

305

End!

Dear Reader,

Wow!

You read five Elephant & Piggie adventures in one book! Congratulations!

Reading every day is a great way to spark your imagination!

When I was a kid, I liked to imagine that I had an Invisible Invention Machine that made Invisible Inventions. My friend Laurie Keller "invented" a drawing of Elephant and Piggie in her own style! It's not invisible, and I love it.

How can you use your imagination to create something new for yourself or Elephant and Piggie?

Your pal,

Mo!

Laurie Keller is the award-winning author and illustrator of *Arnie the Doughnut*, *The Scrambled States of America*, and others. Laurie also wrote and illustrated the Geisel Award-winning ELEPHANT & PIGGIE LIKE READING! book *We Are Growing!*

MO WILLEMS'
ELEPHANT & PIGGIE
LIKE READING!

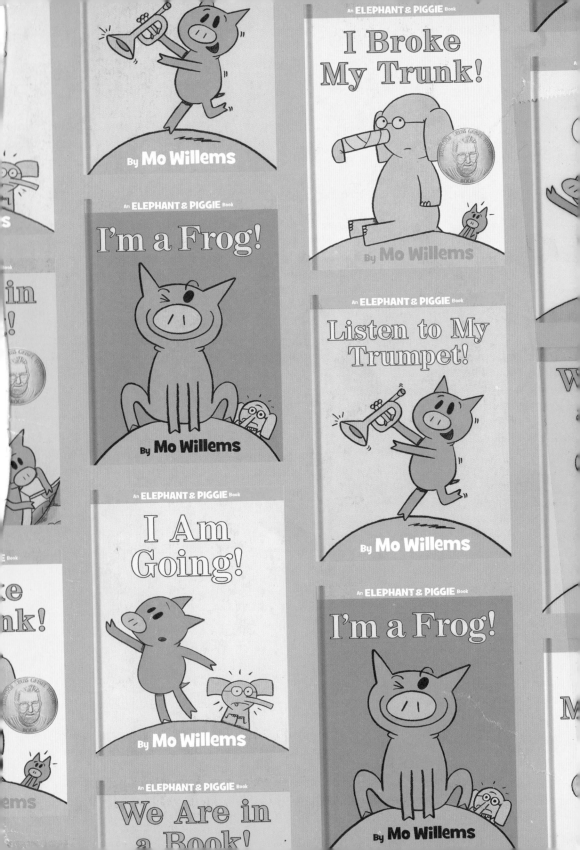